Signed by Santa

Signed by Santa

A Christmas story

By

Mark H. Glissmeyer

Gradina Books

ISBN-13: 979-8-9855771-0-5

Gradina Books

Hi, I am little Joe
and I have a story
you should know.
It all began last year,
after the very first snow.

Christmas was coming
and I wanted this nice toy.
I was good all that year,
and a deserving young boy.

So our house was made ready
and when Santa finally came,
he just passed us right by.
Was I made to blame?

Then I wrote him a letter.
It went to the North Pole.
I had to find out why
and that was my goal.

I didn't hear back
until this very next year.
I hope you are happy
the note said,
in spirit and good cheer.

I'm afraid to tell you why
I missed you that night.
It was even signed by Santa
on paper that was white.

So this is what happened
as best as he said.
He knew where I lived
and how I was sleeping in bed.

He went up on my roof,
but Santa's not very thin.
Yet he still climbed our chimney,
until he couldn't fit back in.

He tried and he tried,
that's what the note said,
until he fell off the top
and it awoke me from bed.

I only saw Santa leaving
and thought he missed me.
Instead, he was off
to climb our neighbor's tree.

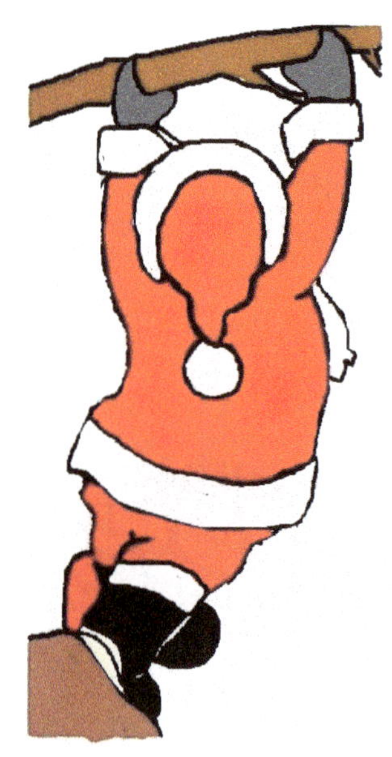

Santa gets lots of mail
that the elves brings to him.
But mine was the letter
that would make him get slim.

Mrs. Claus had found out
and sewn him a smaller suit,
saying he had to work out
and plan a faster route.

He then wanted to return,
but could he make it in time?
He had become way too tired
and could barely even climb.

So he took her advice
and began to lift weights.
He even went out jogging
and slid on ice skates.

He practiced more stretching
and over time he felt fine.
Mrs. Claus saw the difference,
his slimmer waist was the sign.

When the new suit finally fit,
he had gotten back in shape.
Next he planned out the year
and learned the landscape.

There were so many toys,
the effort would be huge.
All the elves must work fast.
He didn't want to be Scrooge.

They read the long list.
Everything must be made.
Things were always rechecked
and all during summer they stayed.

There were boats that needed floating
and electronics needed wires.
Some dolls had some checking
and toy engines rolled their tires.

Only one elf had a gaff
and he ended up with a sprain,
when he fell upside down
while flying a toy plane.

But finally it was finished.
All the toys were complete.
And it happened just in time
since snow fell down our street.

As it snowed and it snowed,
I finally went out with my sled.
I wore some warm mittens
and had a scarf on my head.

I even went down a hill
as fast as I dared.
When I hit the snowbank,
Boy was I scared.

There were others out as well,
making lots of snowballs,
then throwing each of them.
Watching where each one falls.

Others rolled up the snow
into sizes much bigger.
They stacked them together
into very large figures.

One had sticks for the arms
and was a scary snowman.
Another with a broom
became a merry snow-woman.

People also put out wreaths
on many of their doors.
All of them seemed real pretty.
I hope one was on yours.

There was also one man,
he carried some mistletoe.
What it's even meant to do,
I really don't know.

But Santa now knew
that Christmas was coming.
So he came early to town
while singing and humming.

Children sat on his lap
and told him many things.
It was all mostly toys.
What they hope that he brings.

Some had even written down
a long list of it all.
Santa seemed to be thinking
that's very heavy to haul.

But everyone goes away happy,
no matter how long we wait.
To sit on his lap,
we all know he is great.

So after Santa left us,
many had things to prepare.
There were lights to untangle
and hang outside with great care.

Trees were also cut down
and carried into the house.
They picked out a spot
and were helped by their spouse.

Ornaments were now hung up
on their branches with canes.
They kept decorating the trees
and finished all that remains.

Some were even so tiny
they grew in little pots,
with all the small ornaments
making them have tiny spots.

Then carolers came out
to celebrate the good year.
They sang holiday songs
where many of us could hear.

Until finally at last
the night before Christmas came.
Santa was now getting ready
with the list with every name.

He had the reindeer prepared
to pull his big sled.
He made sure they were ready
and each one was well fed.

The toys were bagged up.
He even climbed up one sack,
then tied off the top
and slid down on his back.

This year he had helpers,
the planning that he knew.
Some elves would bring toys.
Even Mrs. Claus helped out too.

I now had gone to bed
after putting out a treat,
some milk and a cookie
for Santa to drink and to eat.

Would he come to my house?
I hope he remembered.
I had sat on his lap
and even written that letter.

Then during the night,
it was like I hoped for.
Down our chimney Santa came
without getting stuck like before.

He came in our house
and placed under our tree
many boxes of presents,
wrapped as pretty as can be.

Then over our large fireplace
our stockings were filled.
They become big and lumpy.
He knew we'd be thrilled.

He left to go on,
so many houses that night.
I never woke up at all
until the morning's first light.

When I looked down the hall,
I knew he'd been back.
The plate with the cookie,
he had eaten the snack!

"HURRAY" I yelled loud,
and woke mommy and dad.
Christmas morning was here.
I sure was real glad!

My little sister got up too.
We all went out to see
the many presents Santa left
all neatly under our tree.

Should we open them now?
Dad picked one right up.
He shook it real quick.
It sounded like a pup.

The rest you can guess
how we tore open things,
after taking off wrappers
and cutting off strings.

Without any Christmas presents
last year was still great,
but now that it's happened,
it was worth the extra wait.

I know that our Christmas
isn't just about toys.
It's also about family
and bringing others joy.

Christmas can't be stopped,
this is what I now know.
Merry Christmas everyone!
Signed, little Joe

www.ingramcontent.com/pod-product-compliance
Lightning Source LLC
Chambersburg PA
CBHW070619310726
48982CB00001B/130

* 9 7 9 8 9 8 5 5 7 7 1 0 5 *